# Tracey and the Sun

Written by Jack Gabolinscy
Illustrated by Ireen Denton

Tracey lived in a new town where the sun shined day after day.

In her old town, there were days of rain or snow, and games inside, and hot chocolate. But in the new place, every day, the sun found some way to annoy her.

One day, she fell asleep under the shade of a tree and the sun sneaked across the sky and took the shade. When she woke, her legs were burned red.

"Look what you've done, Sun!"
she shouted.

On her birthday, Tracey's mom packed her a special cookie. But the sun shined through the classroom window onto her lunch box.

At morning recess, when Tracey went to get her birthday cookie, there was just a pile of melted icing and crumbs.

"Look what you have done, Sun!"
Tracey growled.

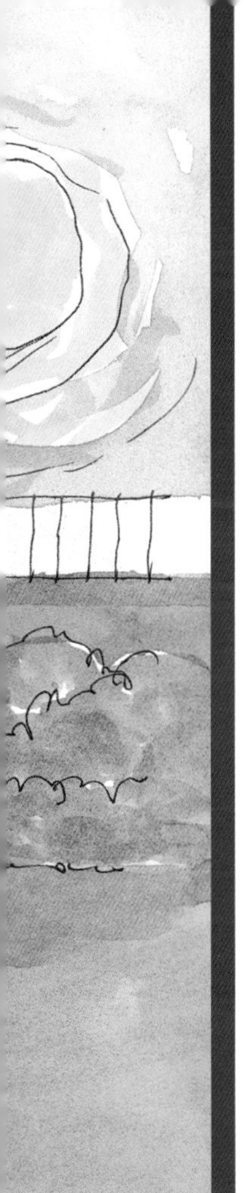

At lunchtime, Tracey played basketball.

She leaped high from the ground to shoot a basket, but the sun shined in her eyes and she missed the point.

She was really angry. She stamped her foot and shook her fist at the sun.

"You spoil everything. Go away!"

Suddenly, Tracey felt cold.

While her friends changed into their swim suits, she put a sweater on.

While her friends splashed and laughed in the pool, she shivered on the pool deck. She wrapped her towel tightly around her to keep warm.

The sun didn't glare into her eyes.

It didn't shine on her shoulders.

It didn't paint her shadow on the wall behind her.

Tracey knew the sun had heard her angry words. She knew now the sun was punishing her.

For the rest of the day, Tracey felt cold. She kept her sweater on, but she could not get warm.

That night, she put three more blankets on her bed. She slept curled up like a cat.

In the morning, Tracey was still cold.

She dressed in her warm clothes.

She sat at the sunny end of the table to eat her breakfast.

She walked to school on the sunny side of the street.

She sat in the sunniest seat in the front of her classroom. But still the sun refused to shine on her.

At morning recess, Tracey sat, cold and shivery, by herself. She watched her friends playing ball in the sunshine. Their happy faces were covered with sunscreen and their hats shaded their heads.

Tracey was sorry she had growled at the sun.

She wished it would shine on her again.

She wished she could feel it warming her skin.

She looked up at the sun. "I'm sorry," she said. "I'm sorry I was nasty and mean."

The sun seemed to look the other way. It did not hear her words.

Just then a little girl fell over and hurt her knee. Tracey ran to help her up.

"There!" she said. "Sit in the sunshine. You'll soon feel a lot better."

All of a sudden, Tracey felt the sun shine on her face. She saw her shadow on the wall. It was as if the sun had seen Tracey's kindness and smiled.

Tracey lifted her face to the sun and smiled back.

"The sun makes everyone happy," she said. And the little girl with the sore knee smiled, too.

# Narratives

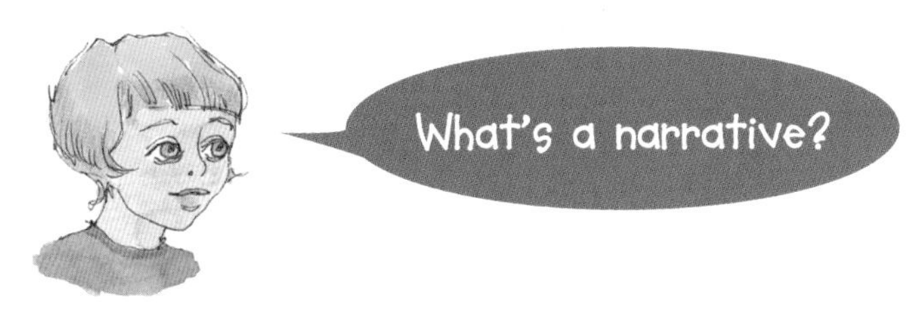


A narrative is a story that has a plot (or storyline) with:

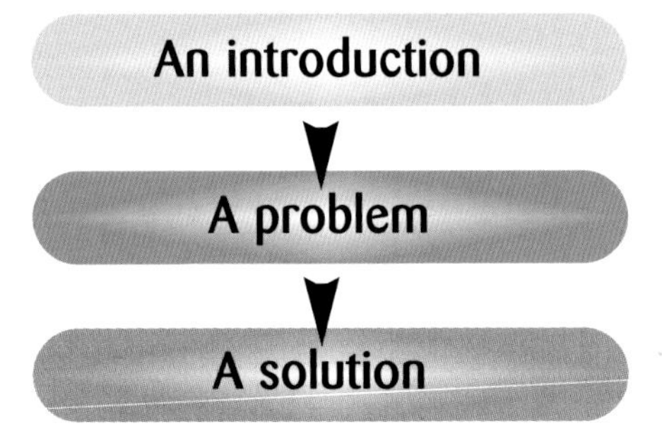


## How to Write a Narrative:

**Step One Write an introduction**
An introduction tells the reader:

- Who the story is about (the characters)
- Where the story takes place (the setting)
- When the story happened

## Step Two **Write about the problem**

Tell the reader about:

- The events in the story and the problems that the main character or characters meet
- What the character/characters <u>do</u> about the problem

> *I told the sun I was sorry*
> *I was nasty and mean.*

## Step Three **Write about the solution**

Tell the reader how the problem is solved.

**Don't forget!**

A narrative can have more than one main character and other characters.

I am the main character.

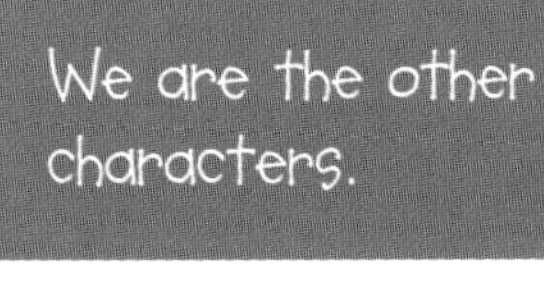

# Guide Notes

**Title: Tracey and the Sun**
**Stage:** Fluency (2)

**Text Form:** Narrative
**Approach:** Guided Reading
**Processes:** Thinking Critically, Exploring Language, Processing Information
**Written and Visual Focus**: Illustrative Text

## THINKING CRITICALLY

(sample questions)

- How do you know that this story is fiction?
- What do you think Tracey could have done to stop her legs from getting sunburned?
- What do you think Tracey could have done to stop the icing from melting on her cookie?
- Why do you think Tracey put three more blankets on her bed and curled up like a cat?

## EXPLORING LANGUAGE

### Terminology

Spread, author and illustrator credits, ISBN number

### Vocabulary

**Clarify:** annoy, shined, gear, punishing, shivery, spoil, fist, refused, glare
**Nouns:** sun, rain, snow, cookie, lunch box
**Verbs:** melt, play, walk, help
**Singular/plural:** leg/legs, cookie/cookies, blanket/blankets, shoulder/shoulders

### Print Conventions

Apostrophes – possessive (Tracey's mom, Tracey's kindness), contraction (didn't, I'm, you'll, you've)

### Phonological Patterns

Focus on short and long vowel **a** (sh**a**de, t**a**ble, c**a**t, **a**t)
Discuss root words – swimming, leaped, slept, sunniest, shook
Look at suffix **ness** (kind**ness**), **ed** (miss**ed**), **ly** (sudden**ly**)
Discuss the silent letter in crum**b**s